S0-EIK-789

EMERGENCY!

By Annie Auerbach
Illustrated by Artful Doodlers

LITTLE SIMON
An imprint of Simon & Schuster Children's Publishing Division
New York London Toronto Sydney
1230 Avenue of the Americas
New York, New York 10020

Manufactured in the United States of America
First Edition
2 4 6 8 10 9 7 5 3 1
ISBN 0-689-86856-1

"9-1-1. What is your emergency?" the dispatcher said on the phone.

Molly was scared. "Uh, my name is Molly Hunter . . . my mommy fell. She's not getting up!"

"Okay, Molly," the dispatcher said. "We're going to help your mommy. What's your address?"

"146 Pinecone Street," replied Molly.

"I'm sending someone right now," the dispatcher told the girl.

Jane and Simon got the call from dispatch. They were emergency medical technicians, or EMTs. Simon turned on the siren in ambulance number 104 and zoomed down the street. Every second counted.

They arrived at Molly's house and carried in a large medical bag, oxygen, and heart monitor. "Mrs. Hunter?" Jane asked, "Do you know where you are? Where does it hurt?"

Jane began to check Mrs. Hunter's temperature, pulse, and blood pressure.

"Where's Molly?" Mrs. Hunter asked. "My leg hurts."

"Molly is right here, Mrs. Hunter, " Simon said.

"I think we have a slight concussion and possible broken leg," Jane said to Simon. "Let's get her on the stretcher."

"Don't worry, Molly," Jane said, "We'll take good care of your mom."

"Mrs. Hunter, you're going to be okay," Jane said. "But we need to take you to the hospital so they can look at your leg."

Molly stayed with a neighbor while her mother was transported to Hero City Hospital.

Before they left, Molly said to Simon, "Thanks for helping my mommy."

Simon bent down and said to Molly, "You are a very brave little girl. You did the right thing."

Inside the ambulance Jane tended to Mrs. Hunter while Simon drove. He alerted the hospital that they were on their way. Cars moved over to let the ambulance through.

Jane squeezed Mrs. Hunter's hand. "You're going to be just fine," she said.

Mrs. Hunter gave her a grateful smile. "Thank you," she said.

"You're welcome," said Jane as they arrived at the hospital. "We're here to help."

AM

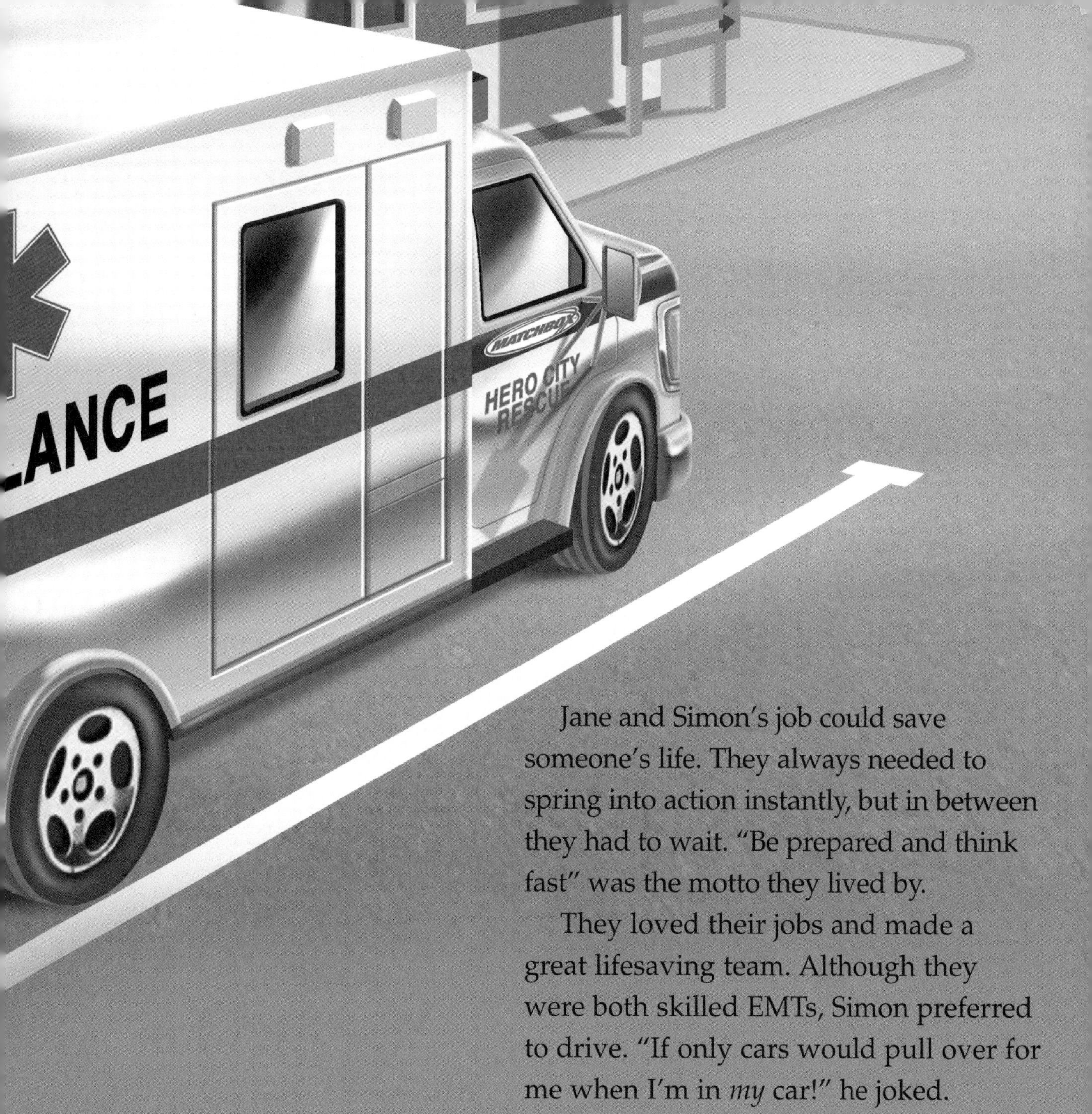

Jane and Simon's job could save someone's life. They always needed to spring into action instantly, but in between they had to wait. "Be prepared and think fast" was the motto they lived by.

They loved their jobs and made a great lifesaving team. Although they were both skilled EMTs, Simon preferred to drive. "If only cars would pull over for me when I'm in *my* car!" he joked.

Just then an emergency call came through from dispatch.
"Dispatch to 104 . . . car pileup on Watson Street near Fourth Avenue."
Simon radioed back, "104 to Dispatch, we're on our way."

Wee-o! Wee-o! The ambulance's siren wailed as the vehicle sped toward the accident site. Even though cars were supposed to pull to the right until the ambulance passed by, Simon had to be extra careful going through intersections. No need for the EMTs to get in an accident too!

Soon the ambulance arrived on the scene. "This looks bad," Jane said. "Let's get to work!"

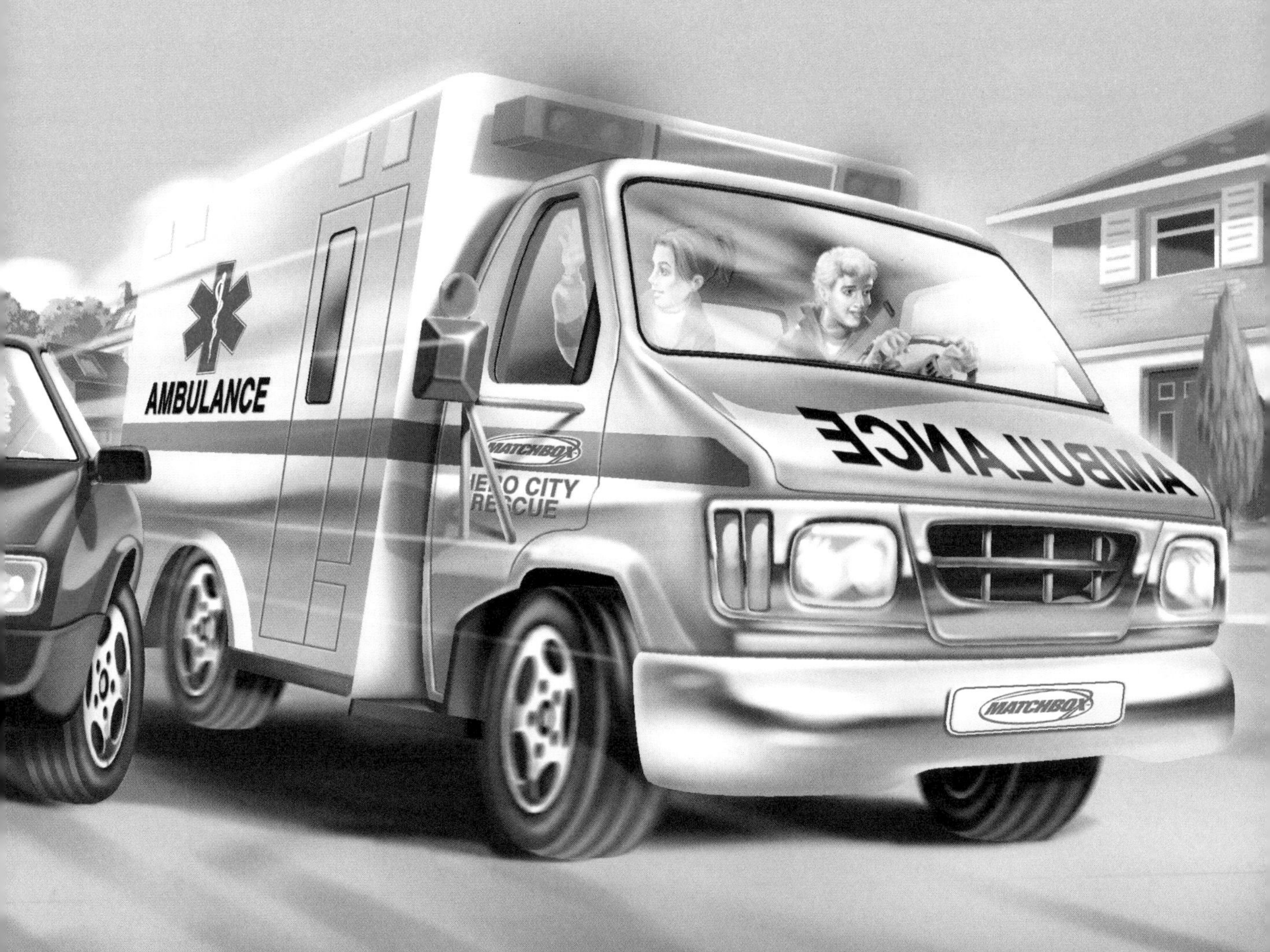

Fire crews, police officers, and EMTs worked together to aid the victims of the multiple vehicle pile-up. Jane tended to a woman who was bleeding, while Simon checked the status of a man who had just been removed from a smashed-up vehicle. The high-speed impact had hurt the man's left knee and arm. He needed to get to a hospital as soon as possible.

But Simon remained calm so as not to alarm the man. "Can you tell me your name, sir?"

"George Webster," the man replied.

Simon said, "Mr. Webster, we're going to take a ride to the hospital."

AMBULANCE

Jane had finished bandaging up the woman when Simon called her over. "We've got to get him to a hospital—and fast!" he whispered in her ear.

They loaded Mr. Webster into the ambulance, and Jane sat in the back, so she could monitor him.

Simon jumped into the driver's seat and started the engine. But there was one *big* problem. Emergencies had no time schedule and it was rush hour!

Horns blared, brakes screeched, and tempers rose. Rush hour in Hero City was challenging for everyday drivers, but Jane and Simon had to get Mr. Webster to the hospital—fast!

Simon had turned on the siren, but because of the accident the backup of cars was so bad that they couldn't move over to let the ambulance through.

"Boy, I wish this ambulance had wings," Jane called out.

"I know," agreed Simon. "But where there's a will, there's a way—even if it's not the normal way!"

Simon steered the ambulance into the center lane that divided the street. It was a dangerous move, but the ambulance's siren would alert oncoming drivers. As an extra precaution for situations such as this one, the word "ambulance" is spelled backward on the front of the ambulance, so drivers can see it correctly in their rearview mirrors.

While Simon was navigating the roads Jane remained in the back, monitoring Mr. Webster. Suddenly Jane noticed he was having trouble breathing. Jane checked his vitals. She couldn't feel his pulse anymore, and she realized the worst: His heart had stopped beating—and they weren't at the hospital yet!

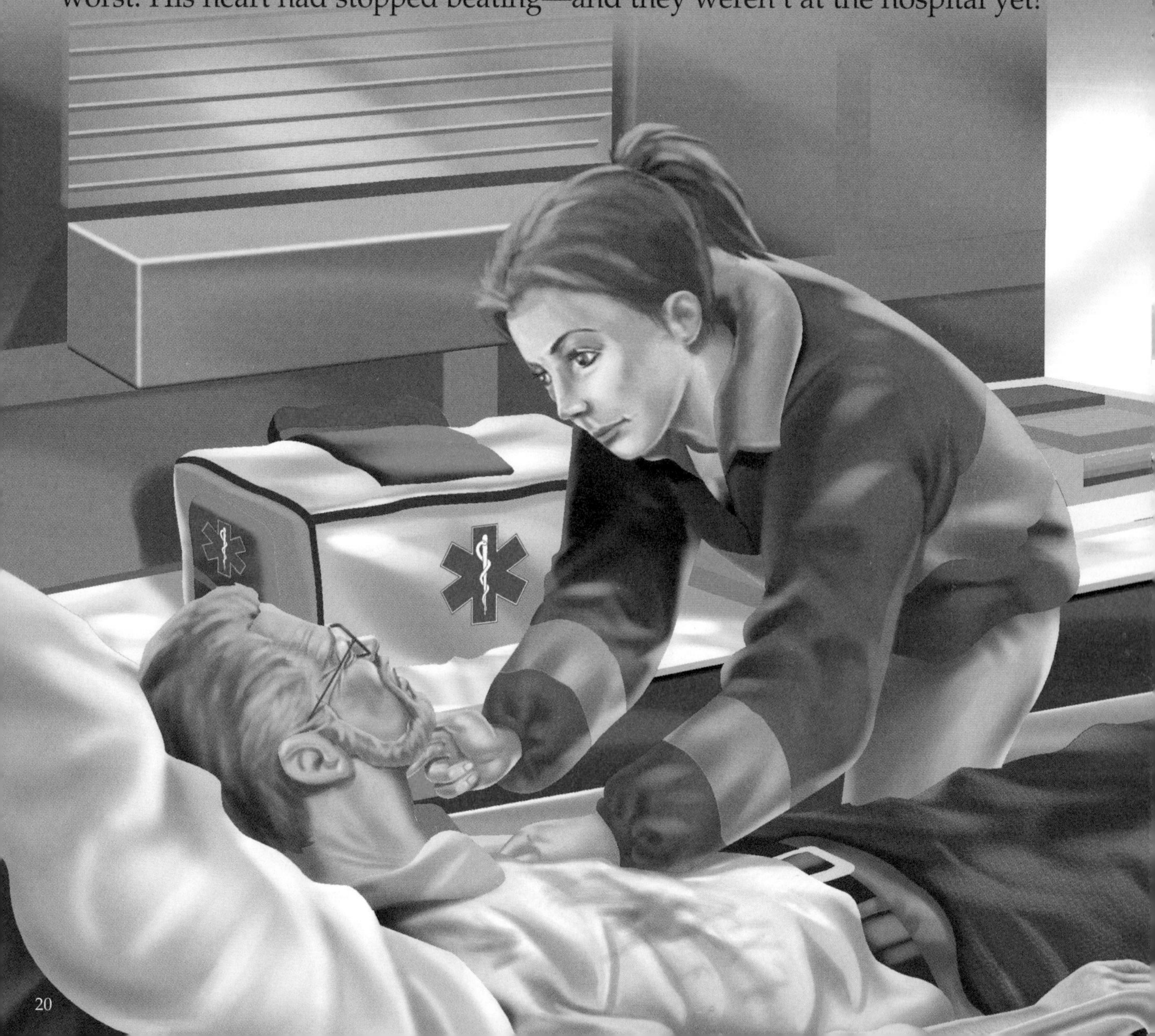

First Jane performed CPR on him, but it wasn't helping. Luckily an ambulance is a lifesaver on wheels. Everything Jane needed to save Mr. Webster's life is in there. Every second is essential! She grabbed a device called an automatic external defibrillator, or AED, that would send electrical shocks to Mr. Webster's heart so that it would start beating again. But would it work in time?

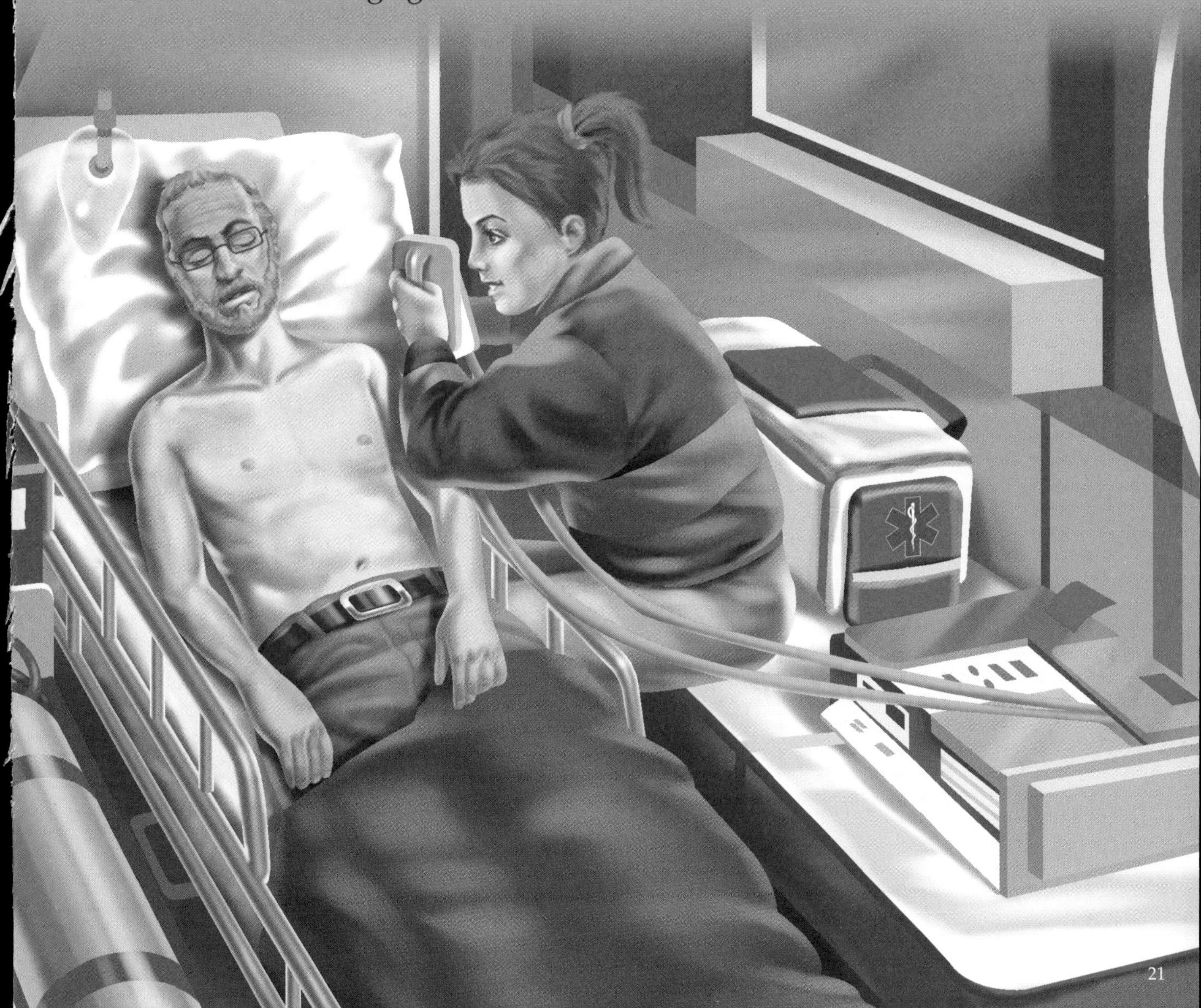

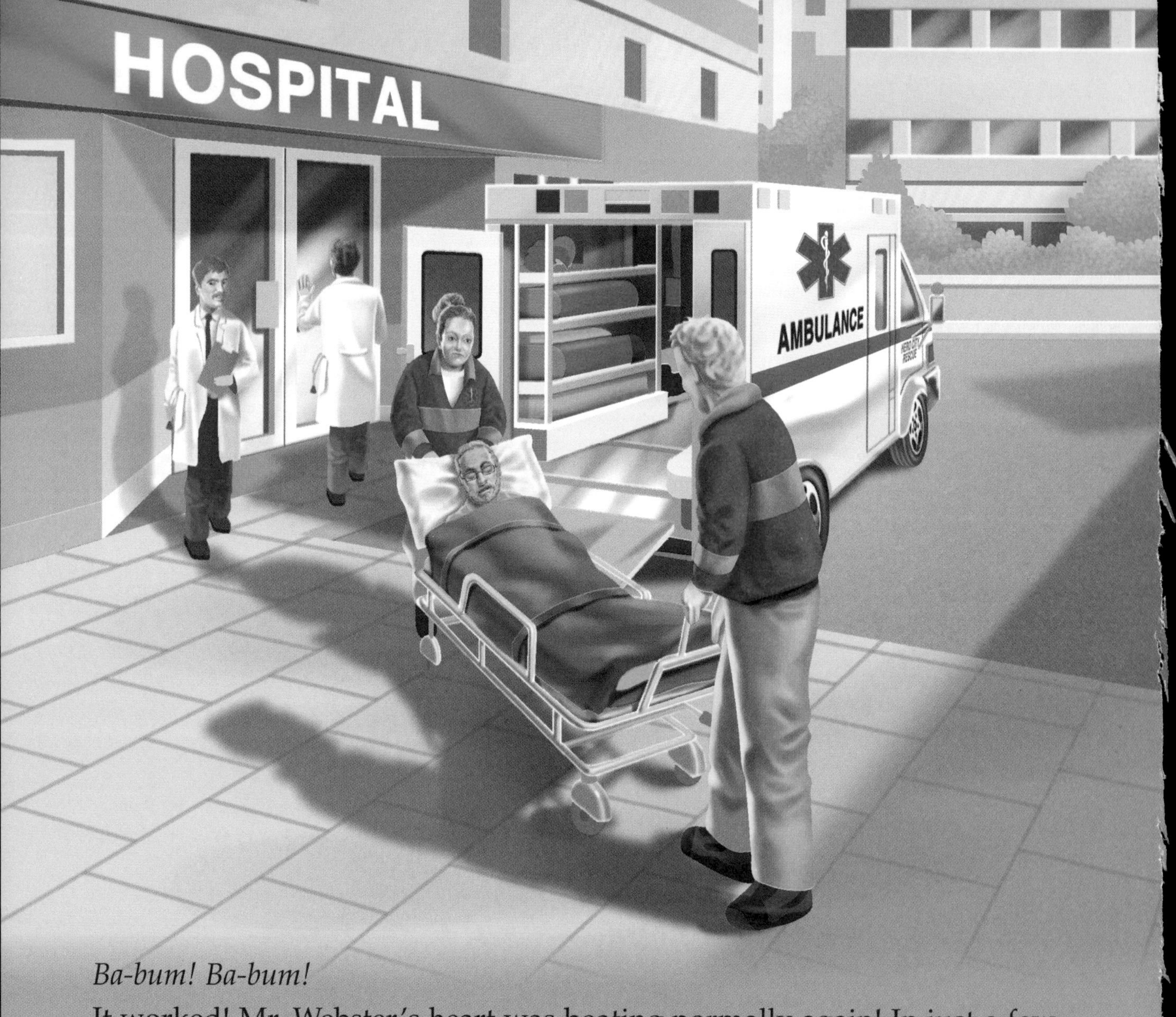

Ba-bum! Ba-bum!

It worked! Mr. Webster's heart was beating normally again! In just a few critical minutes Jane had saved his life.

Once at the hospital Simon leaped out of his seat and helped Jane get Mr. Webster out of the ambulance and into the emergency room.

Leaving the hospital, Simon turned to Jane and said, "Nice work you did!" Jane smiled. "Yeah, it's been a good day."

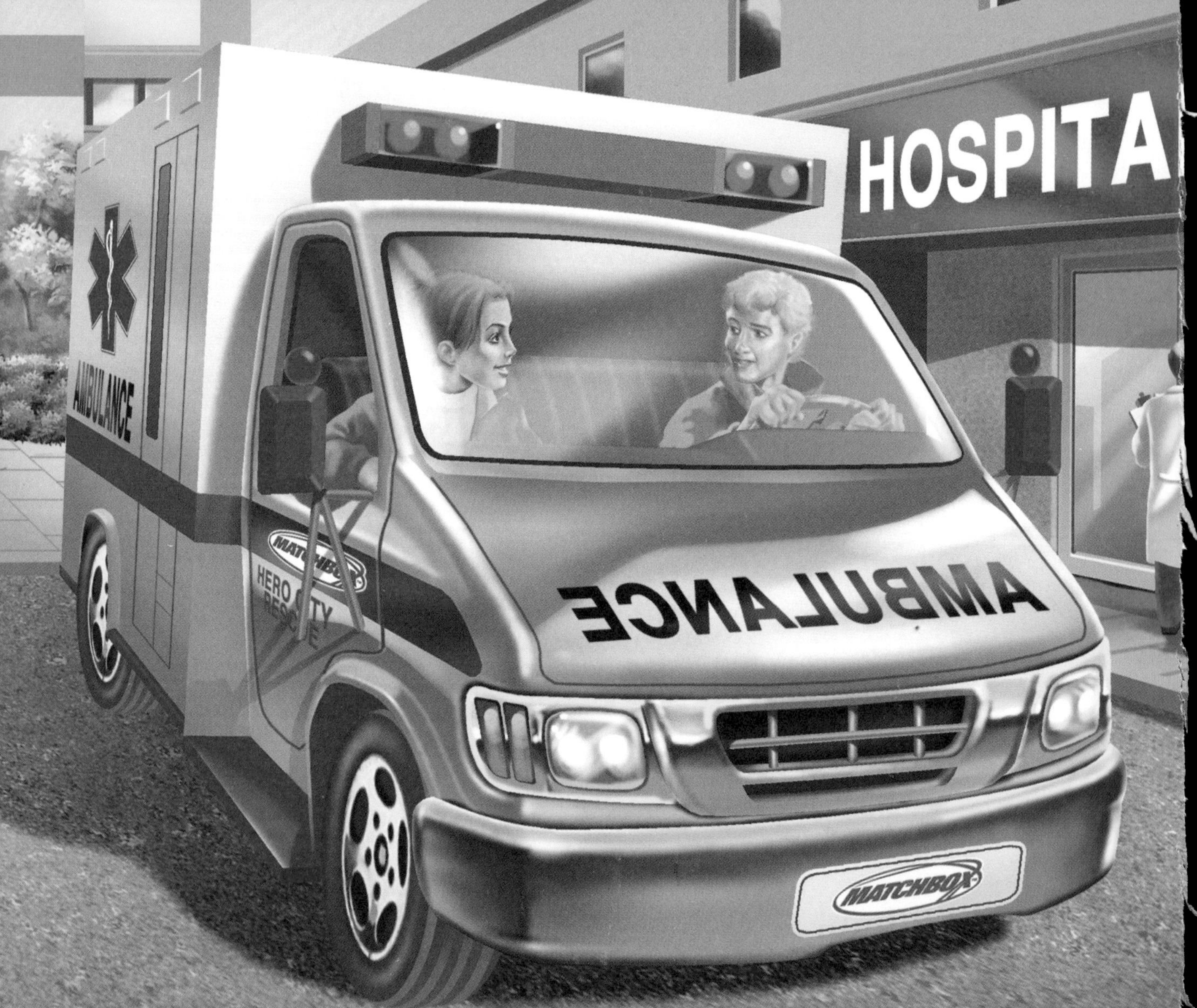

As the pair got back into the ambulance, Jane added, "And nice job on the driving!"

"Just don't tell my son about that little maneuver today!" Simon said with a laugh as they drove off.